STRING QUARTET
IN A MINOR

For Jean on her birthday

R. VAUGHAN WILLIAMS

OXFORD UNIVERSITY PRESS

Time of performance: 20 minutes approximately.

STRING QUARTET IN A MINOR
FOR JEAN ON HER BIRTHDAY

R. VAUGHAN WILLIAMS

I
PRELUDE

NOTE:— In certain passages both dotted and normal slurs appear. In such instances the dotted slur indicates the musical phrasing, while the normal slur shows the bowing.

2

8

II
ROMANCE

poco ritardando

a tempo

III
SCHERZO

IV
EPILOGUE

Greetings from Joan to Jean

26

Reproduced and printed by
Halstan & Co. Ltd., Amersham, Bucks., England

OXFORD UNIVERSITY PRESS